The Intriguing Sources of Hold Your Horses

and Other Idioms

by Arnold Ringstad • illustrated by Dan McGeehan

Published by The Child's World®
1980 Lookout Drive • Mankato, MN 56003-1705
800-599-READ • www.childsworld.com

Acknowledgments
The Child's World®: Mary Berendes, Publishing Director
The Design Lab: Design and production
Red Line Editorial: Editorial direction

Design elements: Kirsty Pargeter/iStockphoto

ISBN 9781614732334
LCCN 2012932811

Printed in the United States of America
Mankato, MN
July 2012
PA02118

Contents

START FROM SCRATCH

MEANING: To **start from scratch** is to start at the beginning without any special advantages.

ORIGIN: The phrase comes from scratching a line in the dirt to mark the starting point of a race. If you start from the scratch you have no advantage.

EXAMPLE: A breeze blew Bronson's homework out the window and into a puddle. Now he would have to **start from scratch**.

SCRAPE THE BOTTOM OF THE BARREL

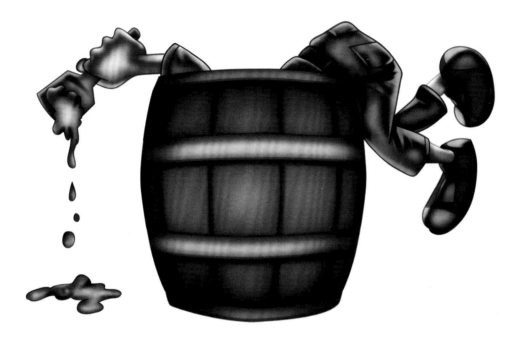

MEANING: If you have to **scrape the bottom of the barrel**, you have to use your last choice for something.

ORIGIN: The phrase comes from storing things such as wine in barrels. Whatever was left at the bottom of the barrel was usually lower quality.

EXAMPLE: The only bananas left at the grocery store were turning brown. It looked like Justina would be **scraping the bottom of the barrel**.

PAINT THE TOWN RED

MEANING: When you **paint the town red**, you have a lot of fun without caring about the consequences.

ORIGIN: The origin of this phrase is uncertain. It may come from an incident in 1837 where a group of men actually painted several buildings red.

EXAMPLE: It was Ben's birthday, and there was no school the next day. He and his friends would **paint the town red** that night.

UPSET THE APPLE CART

MEANING: When you **upset the apple cart**, you create trouble.

ORIGIN: This phrase most likely refers to the disorder caused when an actual cartload of apples spills.

EXAMPLE: Alex **upset the apple cart**. She was absent from school on the day of her group presentation.

ONCE IN A BLUE MOON

MEANING: Something that happens **once in a blue moon** happens very rarely.

ORIGIN: Usually, there is only one full moon each month. When there are two, the second one is known as a blue moon. This happens about once every three years.

EXAMPLE: Once in a blue moon, Meghan drank a soda with lunch instead of her usual vegetable juice.

NIGHT OWL

MEANING: A person who is a **night owl** likes to stay up late at night.

ORIGIN: Originally, *nightowl* was another word for owl. Shakespeare used the word in a poem he wrote in 1594.

EXAMPLE: Cameron was a **night owl**, but only on the weekends.

GET OUT OF DODGE

MEANING: If you **get out of Dodge**, you leave a dangerous place.

ORIGIN: Dodge City, Kansas, was a dangerous town in the late 1800s. Famous gun battles happened there.

EXAMPLE: Cory had to **get out of Dodge**. His mom was cooking his least-favorite dinner, meatloaf.

ON PINS AND NEEDLES

MEANING: When you are **on pins and needles**, you are very nervous.

ORIGIN: A nervous person might have trouble sitting still, as though they are sitting on actual pins and needles.

EXAMPLE: Consuela was **on pins and needles** while she waited to find out her test score.

COVER YOUR BASES

MEANING: If you **cover your bases**, you are fully prepared.

ORIGIN: This phrase comes from baseball. Your players must be ready to make a play at all four bases to stop the other team from scoring.

EXAMPLE: Dan had **covered his bases**. He bought a Father's Day present three months in advance.

BLUE BLOOD

MEANING: A person who is a **blue blood** belongs to a wealthy family.

ORIGIN: This idiom comes from an old Spanish phrase, *sangre azul*. Wealthy families from Spain claimed that they had bluer blood than common people. Actually, their skin was paler. This made their veins more visible so they looked bluer. The phrase was translated into English in the 1830s.

EXAMPLE: Whenever Brenna walked by the country club, she could see the **blue bloods** playing shuffleboard.

KEEP MUM

MEANING: If you **keep mum**, you are being quiet or keeping a secret.

ORIGIN: When a person tries to make noise with his or her mouth shut, the only noise that comes out sounds like "mum."

EXAMPLE: It was hard for Enrique to **keep mum**. He wanted to tell his friend the ending of his new book.

SPICK AND SPAN

MEANING: Something that is **spick and span** is freshly cleaned.

ORIGIN: This originally referred to a new ship. It came from the Old Norse word *span-nyr*, meaning a fresh chip of wood. *Spick* meant spike or nail. The phrase was first used in the 1700s.

EXAMPLE: Tommy cleaned the garage until it was **spick and span**.

PUT YOUR FOOT
IN YOUR MOUTH

MEANING: If you say something embarrassing, you **put your foot in your mouth.**

ORIGIN: In the 1700s, an Irish politician was known for misspeaking. After one incident, another person commented, "Every time he opens his mouth, he puts his foot in it."

EXAMPLE: Victoria **put her foot in her mouth** when she called her teacher "dad."

BREAK THE FOURTH WALL

MEANING: If a character in a fictional story talks directly to the audience, they are **breaking the fourth wall**.

ORIGIN: Many plays are performed on stages with a back wall, two side walls, and a fourth side open to the audience. The open side is considered the fourth wall. Usually it is an imaginary barrier between the actors and the audience.

EXAMPLE: The whole audience laughed when Takeo's character in the play **broke the fourth wall**.

HOLD YOUR HORSES

MEANING: If you **hold your horses**, you are being patient.

ORIGIN: This phrase refers to a way to stop horses from moving by holding their reins.

EXAMPLE: "**Hold your horses**, students!" Ms. Lonetti said. "Don't start the math test until everyone has it."

FLY-BY-NIGHT

MEANING: Someone who is **fly-by-night** is working in a misleading and dishonest way.

ORIGIN: People who were trying to get away with something, such as not paying their rent, would leave town in the middle of the night.

EXAMPLE: Erin thought the new comic book store in town seemed very **fly-by-night**.

FIFTH WHEEL

MEANING: If a person is unwanted in a group, they are a **fifth wheel**.

ORIGIN: On a car, there are only four wheels. A fifth wheel is unnecessary and unwanted.

EXAMPLE: Joe was becoming a **fifth wheel** at the lunch table, so he went to sit with other friends.

DOWN TO THE WIRE

MEANING: If a situation is **down to the wire**, it is not decided until the last possible moment.

ORIGIN: This idiom comes from horse racing. Before cameras were invented, it was hard to tell who won a close race. Judges hung a wire above the track. This made it easier for them to tell which horse passed the finish line first.

EXAMPLE: Omar could tell that the bicycle race would come **down to the wire**.

DRESSED TO THE NINES

MEANING: If someone is **dressed to the nines**, they are dressed in fancy, formal clothes.

ORIGIN: There are many theories about the origin of this idiom. It probably comes from the older phrase "to the nines," meaning perfection. Nine is the highest number with one digit, so it stands for the best.

EXAMPLE: Steven always **dressed to the nines** on the first day of school.

MONEY FOR OLD ROPE

MEANING: Easily made money is **money for old rope**.

ORIGIN: The origin of this idiom is uncertain. It may come from sailors selling rope from their ships after returning to shore.

EXAMPLE: Anything Rosemary earned from the yard sale was **money for old rope**.

A CHIP ON YOUR SHOULDER

MEANING: If you have a **chip on your shoulder**, you have a mean attitude and are looking for a fight.

ORIGIN: This idiom comes from the United States in the early 1800s. If a person wanted to fight, he put a chip of wood on his shoulder. An opponent accepted the challenge by knocking it off.

EXAMPLE: The villain in the movie had a **chip on her shoulder**.

BLOCKBUSTER

MEANING: A play, movie, or book that is very popular is a **blockbuster**.

ORIGIN: The phrase refers to a weapon made by Britain's Royal Air Force in World War II. It was a gigantic bomb that could destroy a whole city block at one time. After the war, movies that had a big impact were called blockbusters.

EXAMPLE: Ben saw his favorite **blockbuster** movie ten times.

OFF THE HOOK

MEANING: If you get **off the hook**, you are getting out of trouble or difficulty.

ORIGIN: This phrase may refer to the idea of a fish getting off a fishhook.

EXAMPLE: Spencer had gotten **off the hook**. His mom thought he had eaten all the ice cream, but his dad admitted to it.

DRY RUN

MEANING: When you practice something, you are making a **dry run**.

ORIGIN: When firefighters in the 1800s practiced their procedures, they didn't actually use water. These practice sessions were known as dry runs.

EXAMPLE: Bryan went on many **dry runs** before he tried to break the world record for tallest house of cards.

TICKED OFF

MEANING: If you are **ticked off**, you are very angry about something.

ORIGIN: The origin of this idiom is uncertain. It may come from the British meaning of "ticking off" things, or crossing them off a list. If you're ticked off at someone, you might tick him or her off your list. Or, it may be an example of people using a common word in place of a swear word.

EXAMPLE: Victoria was **ticked off**. It suddenly got cloudy just when the meteor shower was supposed to start.

BOILERPLATE

MEANING: A standard piece of text that is never changed is **boilerplate**.

ORIGIN: This phrase comes from newspapers in the late 1800s. The printing presses used metal type. Parts of the newspaper that didn't change every day, such as advertisements, were printed using metal plates. The plates were created by pouring boiling lead on a mold.

EXAMPLE: Brittany read the instructions for her new computer game even though it was mostly **boilerplate**.

THE JIG IS UP

MEANING: When **the jig is up**, a scheme or plan is wrecked.

ORIGIN: Today, a jig is a term for a dance. This phrase uses an older meaning for jig: a cheat or a trick.

EXAMPLE: The **jig was up**. Harold's friends saw through his plot to get extra Brussels sprouts at lunch.

DUCKS IN A ROW

MEANING: When you have your **ducks in a row**, you have taken care of your responsibilities.

ORIGIN: The origin of this phrase is uncertain. It likely refers to a mother duck leading her ducklings in a neat row. It may also refer to shooting targets lined up in a row.

EXAMPLE: Arielle wanted to get all of her **ducks in a row** before she went on vacation.

About the Author

Arnold Ringstad lives in Minneapolis, where he graduated from the University of Minnesota in 2011. He enjoys reading books about space exploration and playing board games with his girlfriend. Writing about idioms makes him as happy as a clam.

About the Illustrator

Dan McGeehan loves being an illustrator. His art appears in many magazines and children's books. He currently lives in Oklahoma.